WHAT WAS IT *before it was a chair?*

by Roseva Shreckhise
illustrated by Mina Gow McLean

THE CHILD'S WORLD
ELGIN, ILLINOIS 60120

Distributed by Childrens Press, 1224 West Van Buren Street,
Chicago, Illinois 60607.

Library of Congress Cataloging in Publication Data

Shreckhise, Roseva, 1925-
What was it before it was my chair?

(What was it before—let's find out)
Summary: Describes how a chair is made from a tree.
1. Furniture making—Juvenile literature. 2. Chairs—
Juvenile literature. [1. Furniture making. 2. Chairs]
I. McLean, Mina Gow, ill. II. Title. III. Series.
TS821.S48 1985 684.1'3 85-13238
ISBN 0-89565-326-5

1 2 3 4 5 6 7 8 9 10 11 12 R 91 90 89 88 87 86 85

WHAT WAS IT

before it was a chair?

This is my chair. My mom says it is made of oak. I use it for many things. I stand on it when I want to reach something up high. I hang my clothes on it so I can get dressed quickly in the morning.

But mostly, I sit on my chair. I sit on it when I read a book. I sit on it when I color a picture or work a puzzle.

I wonder how my chair got to be a chair? What was it before it was a chair? Let's find out.

It all starts when acorns fall to the forest floor, sprout roots, and grow. Or, sometimes a person called a forester plants tiny trees which have grown from acorns.

The little trees grow and grow. All summer they grow. They grow for many summers. They keep growing until they are taller than a tall house.

When the trees are finally grown and ready to be cut, the forester marks them with a big X.

Then the tree cutters come to the forest, wearing hard hats and special shoes. They bring a tool with lots of sharp teeth. It is called a *chain saw*.

The workers use the saw to cut the marked trees.

After the trees are cut down, the branches are cut off.

Then the tree cutters cut the trunk into pieces, called logs.

"T i m b e r," the workers shout, as the huge trees crash to the forest floor.

The tree cutters know how to make the trees fall in just the right places, so no one will be hurt.

The logs are put onto large logging trucks. . .

and taken to a sawmill.

There the logs go up a moving slide
into the sawmill and are given a bath.

Next, a machine takes off the tree bark. Another machine slices off the rounded sides of the logs, making them square.

Then the clean logs are cut into boards. The boards are put into a heated building to dry. Fans are used to blow warm air over them.

After the wood is dry, it goes to a mill where a machine makes the boards smooth.

Next the boards are cut into special sizes. Some are cut into parts for chairs. When parts, such as seats, are being cut, boards are put together so more than one piece can be cut at a time.

Round chair legs and other special pieces are cut on a machine called a lathe.

When all the pieces needed for a chair are ready, they are glued together. Clamps hold the pieces in place until the glue is dry.

Then the chair needs to be sanded,

and given a shiny finish.

At last the chair is ready to be sold in a furniture store.

So now I know what my chair was before it was a chair. And the next time you use a wooden chair, you will know that once—long before it was a chair—it was part of a strong tree growing in a forest!

Plus Pages

This is a circle story of what you have read about how chairs are made.

1. Little trees grow in the forest.
2. After many years, the trees are big and strong.
3. Tree cutters take the trees from the forest.
4. At a sawmill, the trees are made into boards.